Fay,
I hope you enjoy
the book!

Julie L. Coe
2/21/09

The Friendship Puzzle

Helping kids learn about accepting and including kids with autism

Written by Julie L. Coe ✚ Inspired by Jennifer Maloni
Illustrated by Sondra L. Brassel

The Friendship Puzzle

Helping kids learn about
accepting and including kids with autism

Written by Julie L. Coe
Inspired by Jennifer Maloni
Illustrated by Sondra L. Brassel

Design and Layout by 5050Design.com

Foreword by Dr. Rebecca Landa,
Director of the Kennedy Krieger Institute's Center for Autism and Related Disorders

ISBN-13   978-0-9789182-4-8
ISBN-10   0-9789182-4-X

The Friendship Puzzle
Julie L. Coe
Price: 14.95

Library of Congress Control Number: 2008932776

For more information about The Friendship Puzzle: www.FriendshipPuzzle.com

Foreword

The story of Mackenzie Mackabee is one that has an important lesson for us all -- that each child is an individual, and each is precious. All children need to know that they fit and are embraced for who they are -- just as they are. And all children have a great deal of potential. For some children, that potential has to be delicately cultivated. Children with autism are among that group. What you see on the surface is not an accurate picture of the child's mind and personality. In order to help children with autism reach their highest potential, we must take time to see the world through their eyes. The better we are at doing that, the more success and fun we will have in our interactions, whether social or academic, with children who have autism.

In recent years, research like that undertaken at the Center for Autism and Related Disorders at the Kennedy Krieger Institute has revealed a lot about autism. We have learned that autism is a spectrum of impairment, ranging from mild to severe. Research has begun to dispel many myths about autism. Myths like "people with autism don't like to be with other people," and "people with autism are not smart," are being replaced with insights that are changing the ability of parents, teachers, and friends to better understand people with autism.

The main characteristic that sets children with autism apart from other children is their difficulty with social interaction. They don't naturally learn how to relate to other people. This can be seen in any number of ways, such as poor eye contact, infrequent response when their name is called, not smiling back when someone smiles at them, not being "polite," or not anticipating other people's needs. It can also be seen in the way they play. They don't naturally know the rules for when to take a turn, how to politely enter into an ongoing game or conversation, how to maintain other people's topic of conversation, how to tell when it is the right time to do or say something, and, in general, how to "read other people's minds" so that they are in sync with the world around them. They need extra time to understand what others are saying, and to formulate their response. They also tend to like things to be very predictable, and can be upset with unexpected change. The way that they perceive sensations -- including sound, sight, smell, touch, and taste -- is often different from other children. This may cause them to squint or cover their ears, or even to become upset at certain sensations.

My experience at Kennedy Krieger has shown me that despite these differences, children with autism are a lot like other children their age. They like toys, they like to chase and be chased, and they like to be accepted by others. Research has shown that children with autism learn best when there is a high level of predictability, when they get meaningful reinforcers for correct responses, and when they are given choices and visual examples of the concepts they are learning. There are techniques that teachers, peers, and family members can learn that will bring out the best in children with autism. This book offers an opportunity for children to gain insight into the world of autism. It also invites them to pause before judging others, and to develop an awareness that things are not always what they seem.

If children adopt Mackenzie Mackabee's way of seeing others, they will create a more compassionate world -- a world where everyone fits.

Rebecca Landa, PhD, CCC-SLP
Director of the Center for Autism and Related Disorders
and of the REACH research program, Kennedy Krieger Institute

WELCOME

My name is Jennifer Maloni. I am not a teacher, a doctor, a therapist or a researcher. I am a mom and I have two beautiful boys, Dominic and Dylan. My hope for them is universal. I want them to be happy, healthy, fulfilled and have lots of friends. I want them to have a good life. But there are obstacles that must be overcome. My children live in a world that few understand. It could easily be a world without communication, friendship, or love. It could easily be a world without hopes and dreams. It is my job to make sure that does not happen. Dominic and Dylan have autism, but I will not let it have them.

A while back, my son Dylan and I were at a party. Some kids were playing soccer. My little boy, who has so few words, ran over and grabbed the ball and started running. My first reaction was an overwhelming sense of joy. He wanted to play. This was wonderful. I wanted to jump up and down. He was trying to make friends! And then I realized that the other kids didn't understand. They thought Dylan was trying to take their ball. Instead of fostering new friendships that day, I ended up leaving the party feeling sad and disheartened. I wish I hadn't left. It could have been a wonderful teaching moment for all of us if I had just said, Dylan wants to play but he doesn't know how to tell you.

It got me thinking that what we need to do is raise a generation of children who understand and care about this disorder. I want my children to have friends, to be embraced and to be included. I know that it is difficult to explain to a child about autism and I realize that it can be even harder to show them how to be friends with kids who are different. There is no simple explanation. Many people just do not know quite what to say, how to interact, how to engage and foster these relationships. But I do and I can share this with you.

Autism is a puzzle. We do not know its cause. We do not have its cure. And there is
no easy way to teach others about this disorder. My hope is that this book is a start. That it will generate discussions and lead to teaching moments during which we can all show our children how to embrace others, even those who seem different. We CAN NOT let this generation forget their peers.

Together, we can raise a generation who WILL NOT judge those with special needs but rather, who WILL embrace them, understand them, and include them. If we can change our children's perception, we can change the future. If every child is taught about autism and other disorders and is helped to understand how to be friends with those who are different; if we do this, then we grow a whole generation of friends -- people who know how to be good to one another. This is my hope.

DEDICATION

This book is dedicated to Dominic and Dylan Maloni and all those who are living with autism. May you experience the joy and happiness that comes with the gift of true friendship.

And to our families and friends who supported us in this project, thank you for your love and encouragement.

PS: Thank you Gamb for the brilliant title!

My name is Mackenzie Mackabee. I go to school at Brook Acres Elementary.

I have the best teacher ever. Her name is Ms. Noonan. I love school.
I also love to meet new people and make new friends. But sometimes, you meet a
new person who doesn't seem like a friend. Like, you might meet a boy and think
he's really mean because he doesn't talk to you. Or, you might meet a girl you
think is not very nice because she won't throw
around the ball with you. My mom
says that sometimes friendship is like a
puzzle. You have to step back and see
how all the pieces fit. So when I met
Dylan, the new boy at school, and he
seemed a little different, I decided to
find out how to be his friend.

On the first day of school, I said hello to Dylan but he didn't answer.

He went right to the back of the classroom and sat down. Now he sits back there everyday. He likes to hum to himself. He's usually really quiet, but sometimes I see him waving his hands around, and one time, right in the middle of class, he made this really loud, funny noise.

I wonder why?

At lunch time our cafeteria can get really loud.

Dylan sometimes puts his hands over his ears like he doesn't like all the noise. Maybe it hurts his ears? Maybe he just wants to be alone? I know sometimes I get in a bad mood and don't want to talk to anyone. Maybe that's it. I wish I knew.

During recess, a bunch of us play soccer.

I really wanted Dylan to play with us but when I asked him, he didn't answer me. He just likes to swing on the swings. Sometimes, he stays on the swings FOREVER. Even when it's someone else's turn he doesn't share. He just stays by himself. Maybe he doesn't have any friends?

This makes me feel really sad because everyone needs friends, don't they?

Then, one day, right in the middle of our soccer game, Dylan ran over and grabbed our ball.

He started running and running (he was really fast!). Everyone started shouting, "Dylan took the ball and won't give it back!" And, "He's ruining the game, make him stop!" I don't know why, but I just had this feeling that he wasn't trying to ruin our game.

I tried to tell everyone that I didn't think he wanted to ruin the game but no one heard me. Just then I saw Ms. Noonan, so I ran over to tell her what was happening.

Ms. Noonan put her hand on my shoulder and said,
"Mackenzie, I am so glad that you asked me. I don't think Dylan
is trying to ruin your game either. I think he wants to play and doesn't
know how to tell you." I asked her why he couldn't just say so. Then Ms.
Noonan told me that Dylan has something called "autism." She said that
he doesn't have a lot of words and that it is hard for him to tell people he
wants to play or be friends. "Imagine that you really wanted to play with
the other kids but didn't know how to tell them," she said.

I thought about this for a while and then I told Ms. Noonan that it would be really hard if I couldn't just say it.

I asked Ms. Noonan if that was also why Dylan does things like making funny noises in class and putting his hands over his ears during lunch and not looking at you when you say hello. Ms. Noonan gave me a big smile and said that is exactly why. Now it was starting to make sense to me.

Ms. Noonan suggested that we get some soccer balls and show Dylan how to play.

I thought that was a great idea. So we took the soccer balls out to the field. Dylan still had our ball and was holding it tight. "Hey," I called to everyone. "I think Dylan wants to play with us but he has never played soccer before. Let's show him." Everyone started kicking the balls around.

Then I kicked one to Dylan, and when he kicked it back
it went so far that it flew all the way across the field.
That was the farthest I ever saw a soccer ball go!

Everyone started cheering
and when I looked over at
Dylan, he had a big smile
on his face!

Recess is a lot more fun now. Some days Dylan and I just sit on the swings and swing forever.

Other days, we play soccer. Dylan has been practicing and he is really good! And he can run faster than anyone on the field. When we pick teams, everyone wants Dylan. He always gets picked first! But I think his favorite thing is being with me because he gets the biggest smile when we are on the same team and so do I! He still doesn't say much but now I know why, so I find ways to be with him. I save him a seat at lunch and we walk together to the bus. It was like my mom said.

It was a puzzle and I just had to figure out how the pieces fit.

About this book

Thank you so much for reading this book. We hope you liked it. It was written for enjoyment but we also hope that you will use it as a tool to stimulate open discussion with your children. Autism is so prevalent that it is likely to touch everyone's life at some point or in some way. Our goal is to raise a generation of children who understand and care -- care about this disorder, care about those who seem different, care about others in general. All it takes is a little knowledge and a lot of love! Autism is already such a mystery. Being friends with an Autistic child shouldn't be!

We believe in the importance of creating an environment in which children are encouraged to ask questions and feel comfortable talking about issues. We want children to know that it is OK to ask.

The following activities are designed to open up the lines of communications. They are activities intended to engage kids and help them focus on understanding similarities and differences as well as practicing inclusion. We hope you will try some and if you come up with new ideas, please share them with friends, family, co-workers and us!

Suggested activities

For one week, assign a buddy to a child with autism. That person will be his recess buddy, lunch buddy, circle buddy, etc. During that time, the buddy makes sure the child with autism is included.

Get a really large floor puzzle and separate the pieces. Ask the children what they think the puzzle is. Then, have them work together to figure out where the pieces go and then see what the puzzle really is! (Lesson: Sometimes what we first think we see is not really what we see.)

More activities

Play a game of "likes and differences." Have two kids come up to the front of the room. Ask what is different about them -- For eXample, "What is different about Susie and Billy?" Then ask, "What is the same?" (Lesson: We have some things that make us different, but we all have things that make us the same.)

Engage the class in inclusion-type activities. For eXample, pair a child with autism with a "typical" child. Have them take turns tracing each other's hands or playing a game like kick the ball.

Pick a partner for each child in the class. (Have the assigned buddy paired with the child with autism). Have the children **visualize activities** or games that they would like to play with their partner. Then have them draw a picture of the activity they want to do. Hang the pictures on a bulletin board in the classroom. This serves as a visual reminder to include others.

Focus on activities where children are **rewarded** for taking turns. (For example, "First I will go to the blackboard and draw a picture. Then, you will go to the blackboard and add to the picture.") When rules are followed, give lots of praise (way to go, high five, etc.)

Discussion Questions

1. What are some of the things that Mackenzie notices that Dylan does in class?

2. Why do you think he does these things?

3. Why do you think Dylan doesn't answer Mackenzie when she asks his name or asks him to play soccer?

4. Why did the other kids think Dylan was trying to ruin their game?

5. Why do you think Dylan grabbed the ball instead of asking if he could play?

6. What are some things that Dylan does really well in the book?

7. Aside from soccer, what other things can Mackenzie and Dylan do together?

8. In what ways can the other kids help Dylan at school?

9. Why did Mackenzie say that recess became more fun?

10. How can you make someone in YOUR class feel welcome?

Remember, praise can be a powerful tool.

Always give praise when **you** see children reaching out to others --
especially when they do it all on their own ("Betsy, that was so nice of **you**
to walk with Dylan to lunch. **You** are so thoughtful!")

About the Author

Julie Coe is an avid reader and lifelong lover of literature who has always dreamed of writing children's books. She spent many hours during her youth daydreaming about her books, creating characters and writing stories. She put this dream on hold for the next few decades while she completed school, including earning a BS in Journalism and a MEd in Counseling and Personnel Services at the University of Maryland College Park. Upon completing her bachelor's degree, she began working at University of Maryland University College. She has spent the pas 18 years there assisting students in achieving their higher education goals.

It was not until the birth of her son in October 2004, that she resumed writing children's stories in earnest. Following the birth of her daughter in November 2006, she began pursuing the publication of her manuscripts.

In early 2008, she collaborated with two long-time friends: Jenny Maloni, the moth of two children with autism, and Sondra Brassel, a lifelong artist, to create the book "The Friendship Puzzle: Helping kids learn about accepting and including kids with autism." They have spent the past year working with the staff at Larstan Publishing as well as many other talented individuals, to get the book from initial concept to print.

In addition to this book, Julie has created a number of other children's books that she hopes to publish. In the near future, she also plans to work with Jenny and Sondra on a follow-up book to "The Friendship Puzzle."

About the Illustrator

Sondra Brassel has been painting and drawing since childhood. She has continued to pursue her love of drawing, earning a BS degree in 1989 from the University of Maryland College Park School of Design and an MS degree in 1994 in Urban Studies and Planning.

She was employed as an analyst at The Federal Home Loan Mortgage Corporation for six years. She then retired from FHLMC to raise her children and to revisit her creative talent. In addition to raising her two boys, Alex and James, her spare time is spent drawing and painting.

In 2007, at the request of her long-time friend Julie Coe, Sondra agreed to begin doing illustrations for some of Julie's children's books. Then, in spring of 2008, she received the call to help with a new children's book project dealing with autism. Given the importance of this topic, her friendship with Julie Coe and Jenny Maloni, and her love of drawing, Sondra quickly agreed to join the team. "The Friendship Puzzle: Helping kids learn about accepting and including kids with autism" is her first book of published illustrations. Sondra looks forward to future projects in illustrating.

For additional information on the book, fun activities, and autism resources, please visit our website at:

www.friendshippuzzle.com
Thank you!

On our website, there is a link to the IAN video, which features Dominic and Dylan Maloni. We encourage you to check out the video and the IAN Project website http://www.ianproject.org/ (or click on http://www.friendshippuzzle.com/ and go to The Resources page).

IAN Project Information

The Interactive Autism Network (IAN) is an innovative online initiative that links parents and researchers to accelerate and coordinate autism research. Launched in April 2007 by the Kennedy Krieger Institute, with funding from Autism Speaks, the IAN Project has quickly become the largest collection of autism data in the world and an invaluable resource for the autism community. The IAN Project thanks the Maloni family for the support they have shown through joining the initiative in its earliest phase and helping to increase awareness by appearing in a national public service announcement. By sharing their personal motivation for participating in the IAN Project, they helped to spur nearly 30,000 others to join them.

It is the hope of the IAN Project, the Kennedy Krieger Institute and the Maloni family that families and individuals with Autism Spectrum Disorders can join with researchers, therapists, educators, and other professionals in the autism field to better understand this complex disorder and to develop effective strategies that will improve the lives of people on the spectrum.

We all have questions ... together we'll find answers.
Learn more at www.IANproject.org.